A Pal for Pugwug

To my very dear friend, Neil Mountain, with love
S.J-P.
To my mother, Ella Macnaughton
T.M.

School Specialty.
Publishing

This edition published in the United States in 2006 by Gingham Dog Press,
an imprint of School Specialty Publishing, a member of the School Specialty Family.

A Pal for Pugwug

By Susie Jenkin-Pearce

Illustrated by Tina Macnaughton

GINGHAM DOG
PRESS

Columbus, Ohio

Pugwug was slipping and sliding along, when–*Bang!*–he bumped into a big group.

But no one paid any attention to him.
What were all the penguins looking at?
Pugwug just had to know!

He bounced...

He flapped...

He tried diving through a tiny gap...

...but it was no use.

Finally, Big Penguin turned around.
On his feet rested something large
and round.

"Pugwug," said Big Penguin, "meet your new little brother—or maybe your sister!"

Pugwug shrieked with delight. "Come on," he yelled, "let's play!"

But Pugwug's little pal
did not seem to want to play.

Pugwug tried to make his little pal
look more like a brother—or sister!

But he made a bit of a mess.
"Pugwug, remember to be gentle,"
said Big Penguin.

"Come on, let's race!"
said Pugwug, squealing.

"Or let's play catch!" shouted Pugwug.

"No-no, you must be gentle," reminded Big Penguin.

"I know! How about football?" said Pugwug.

"No football!" warned
Big Penguin anxiously.

Suddenly, one of the penguins shouted, "Danger! Seal alert! Penguin in trouble!"

"Pugwug," said Big Penguin worriedly, "look after our egg. Watch, but **don't touch!**" Then, Big Penguin flapped away as fast as he could.

Pugwug and his little
pal were all on their own.
Suddenly, the egg began
to wobble and shake...

and tumble and roll!

Pugwug didn't
know what to do!

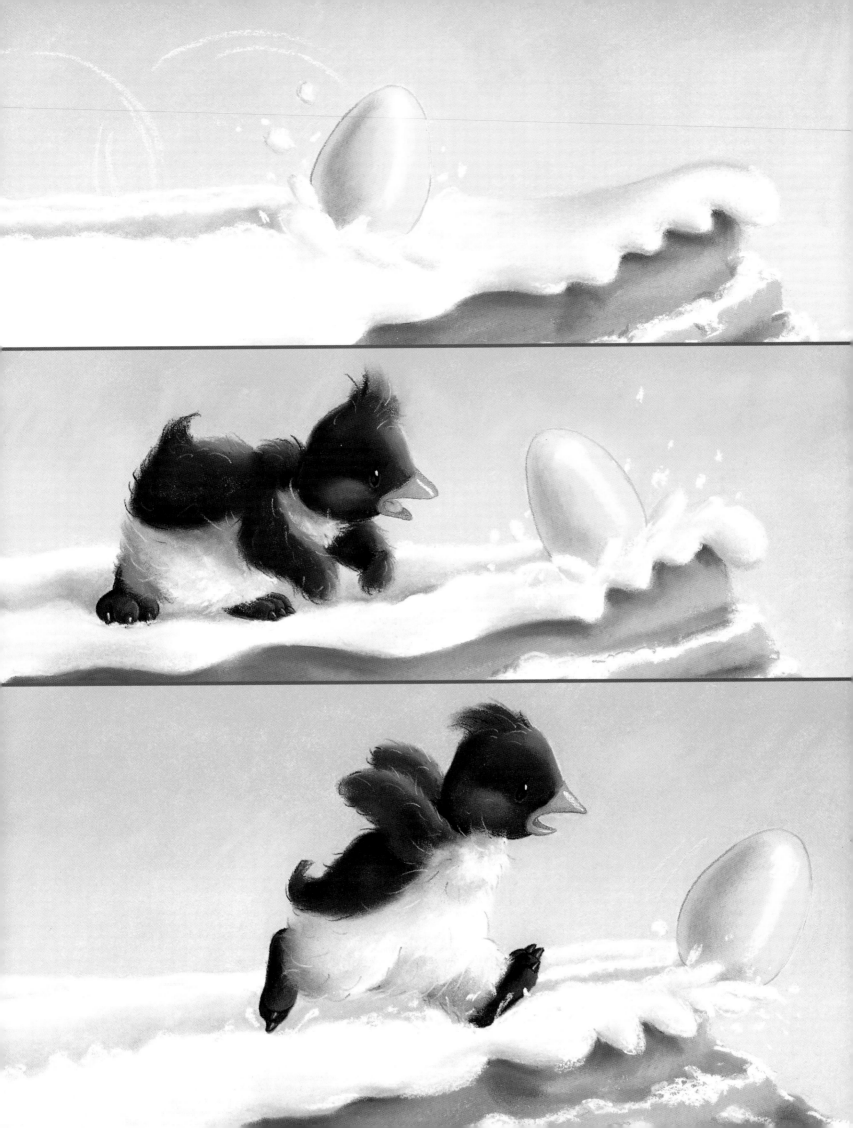

But then, he realized that he **had** to touch!

Pugwug lunged
after his little pal
and held on tightly.

And then...

When Big Penguin returned, he found
Pugwug and his new little pal snuggling.
"Big Penguin," said Pugwug, "meet my
new baby sister!"